Finding a Dove
for Gramps

Lisa J.
Amstutz

PICTURES BY
Maria Luisa
Di Gravio

Albert Whitman & Company
Chicago, Illinois

Mom and I slip silently out the door.
Today we're going to count birds.
It's just the two of us this year,
since Gramps flew south for the winter.
"Just like the swallows!" he said.

Gramps loves birds, and I do too.
Doves are his favorite.
This year, I want to find a dove for Gramps.

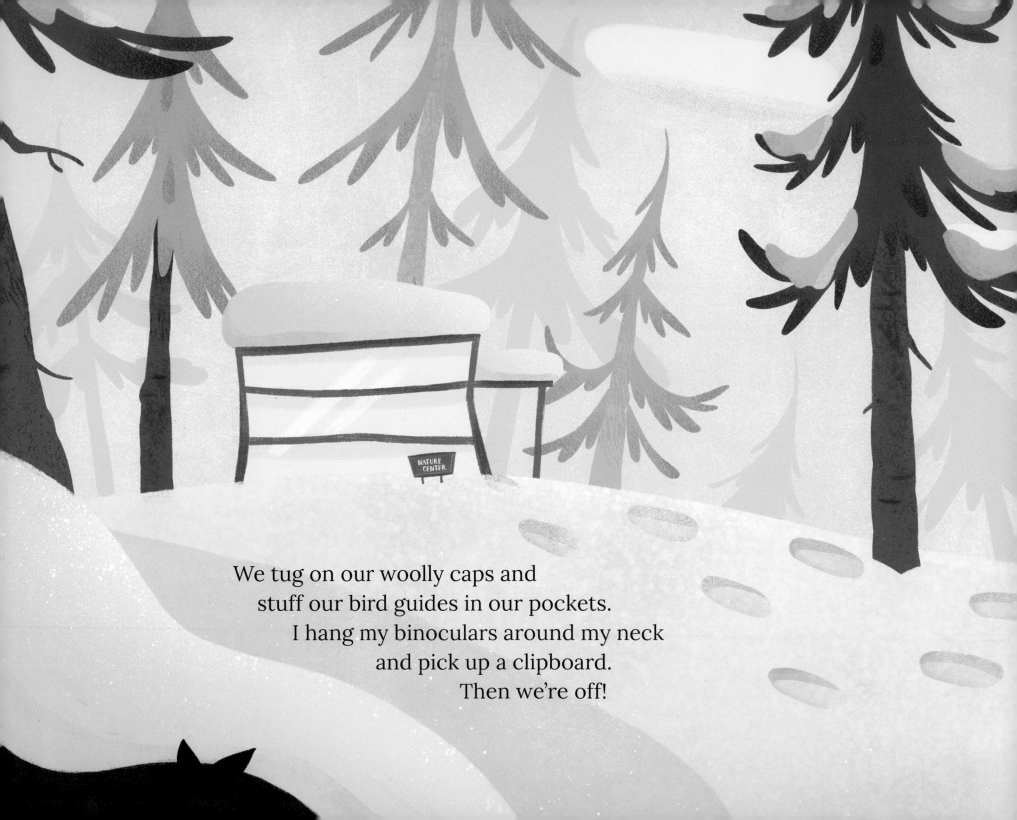

We tug on our woolly caps and
stuff our bird guides in our pockets.
I hang my binoculars around my neck
and pick up a clipboard.
Then we're off!

Mom and I set out toward the big pond.
The spicy smell of pine makes my nose tingle.
I walk lightly, so I won't scare the birds,
snow crunching ever-so-softly underfoot.

It isn't long 'till we hear a call: *Jeer! Jeer!*

I lift my binoculars to my eyes,
just like Gramps taught me.

There—a splash of blue in the
tangled branches.
A blue jay! And another!
I mark my sheet.

Mom says people have been counting birds
for over a hundred years.
"Whoa," I say. "That's—"
Mom puts her finger to her lips.
I freeze like a statue.
All I hear is the wind.
Shhhhhhhhhh...

And then...

Rat-a-tat-tat-tat!
A red-bellied woodpecker hammers a drumroll
at the top of a dead oak tree.
I find his name on the list. *Check.*

Crunching on through the snow, we scare up a gray bird.
My heart jumps. A dove?

No, too small.

It's a tufted titmouse, all dressed up
in his suit and top hat,
as Gramps always says.

Looking up, I spot a flash of yellow. I point silently.

Mom follows my finger to a white pine dripping with icicles.
Her eyes crinkle in a smile. "Golden-crowned kinglet," she whispers.
"Cool!" I whisper back.
That's one we haven't seen before.
Then I notice another yellow spot.
I check my bird guide.
A yellow-rumped warbler!
Check. Check.

Chickadees dart overhead.
Chickadee-dee-dee, they call.
The forest is fully awake now.

Another bird skitters headfirst
down the raggedy trunk
of a hickory tree.
"Must be a nuthatch," I say.
Mom nods. "Gramps taught you well!"

The *squonk squonk* of Canada geese tells us the pond is near.
My head itches under my hat, and I can't feel my pinkie toes.
I stomp my feet to warm them.
"Should we head back?" Mom asks.

"No way," I say. "I want to finish counting."
And not only for Gramps. Or me.

The Bird Count tells scientists
how the birds are doing,
so they can protect them
in the future.

Finally, we arrive at the pond.
A flock of mallards waggle their tails at us.
I pull out my bird guide to identify
a black-and-white duck with a colorful head
and a blue-gray bird on stilts.

Bufflehead.
Great blue heron.

Check. Check.

Mom looks at her watch. "Time to go," she says.
I sigh.
No doves this year, I guess.
I miss Gramps more than ever.

Back at the nature center, we turn in our checklist.
I wrap my hands around a steaming cup of hot chocolate.
My fingers prickle as they start to warm up.
Our leader tallies the lists
and posts the results on the board.

Altogether, the group has counted seventy species.
That's five more than last year!
Everyone claps and cheers.
We say our good-byes
and turn to go.

And that's when I see a flash
of pearly gray on the windowsill.

The dove bobs its head,
and I nod back.

A smile spreads across my face.
I can't wait to tell Gramps!

About the Christmas Bird Count

In the late nineteenth century, many Americans took part in a "Side Hunt" after Christmas dinner each year. The hunter with the biggest pile of dead animals was declared the winner of the hunt. The conservation movement was just beginning at the time, and a man named Frank Chapman proposed the Christmas Bird Count as an alternative to the Side Hunt. Chapman was an ornithologist, or bird scientist, and an officer of the Audubon Society, an organization whose mission is to protect birds and their habitat. He also worked as Curator of Birds at the American Museum of Natural History. Thanks in part to Chapman's vision, the Christmas Side Hunt died out as a new interest in conservation grew.

The first Christmas Bird Count, or CBC, as it's often called, took place in 1900. Twenty-seven people across twenty-five locations counted a total of ninety species. Today, counts take place in over 2,400 locations in North, Central, and South America, with tens of thousands of people counting a total of more than 2,000 species each year. The counts take place between December 14 and January 5. Many people now use the eBird Mobile app to track their sightings throughout the year.

The Christmas Bird Count has become an important way of tracking the status of bird populations and the effects of climate change. Along with other surveys, it shows how bird populations have changed over the past one hundred years. Scientists can use this data to determine the best way of protecting bird species and their habitats.

Want to Join a Bird Count?

Visit the Audubon website (http://www.audubon.org) for a list of count circles near you. Not all bird counts are open to children, so be sure to check with the leader first. Some areas host special Christmas Bird Count events for kids. If there isn't one in your area, consider starting your own! Instructions and materials are available at the Sonoma Birding website. (http://www.sonomabirding.com)

Can't make it to a count during the holidays? Join the Great Backyard Bird Count in February or one of the many other citizen science projects that take place throughout the year. Or visit eBird.org to do your own bird count any day of the year!

Bird Count Checklist

DUCKS, GEESE, AND SWANS
- ☐ American Black Duck
- ☐ Bufflehead
- ☐ Canada Goose
- ☐ Common Goldeneye
- ☐ Common Merganser
- ☐ Gadwall
- ☐ Hooded Merganser
- ☐ Mallard
- ☐ Redhead
- ☐ Wood Duck

NEW WORLD QUAIL
- ☐ Northern Bobwhite

PARTRIDGES, GROUSE, TURKEYS, AND OLD WORLD QUAIL
- ☐ Ring-necked Pheasant
- ☐ Wild Turkey

BITTERNS, HERONS, AND ALLIES
- ☐ Great Blue Heron

KITES, HAWKS, EAGLES, AND ALLIES
- ☐ Bald Eagle
- ☐ Cooper's Hawk
- ☐ Northern Harrier
- ☐ Red-shouldered Hawk
- ☐ Red-tailed Hawk
- ☐ Rough-legged Hawk
- ☐ Sharp-shinned Hawk

PIGEONS AND DOVES
- ☐ Mourning Dove
- ☐ Rock Pigeon

KINGFISHERS
- ☐ Belted Kingfisher

WOODPECKERS
- ☐ Downy Woodpecker
- ☐ Hairy Woodpecker
- ☐ Northern Flicker
- ☐ Pileated Woodpecker
- ☐ Red-headed Woodpecker
- ☐ Red-bellied Woodpecker

FALCONS
- ☐ American Kestrel

PERCHING BIRDS

Jays, Magpies, and Crows
- ☐ American Crow
- ☐ Blue Jay

Larks
- ☐ Horned Lark

Chickadees and Titmice
- ☐ Black-capped Chickadee
- ☐ Tufted Titmouse

Nuthatches
- ☐ Red-breasted Nuthatch
- ☐ White-breasted Nuthatch

Creepers
- ☐ Brown Creeper

Wrens
- ☐ Carolina Wren
- ☐ Winter Wren

Kinglets
- ☐ Golden-crowned Kinglet

Thrushes
- ☐ American Robin

Mockingbirds, Thrashers, and Allies
- ☐ Northern Mockingbird

Starlings
- ☐ European Starling

Waxwings
- ☐ Cedar Waxwing

Longspurs and Snow Buntings
- ☐ Snow Bunting

Wood Warblers
- ☐ Yellow-rumped Warbler

New World Sparrows and Allies
- ☐ American Tree Sparrow
- ☐ Dark-eyed Junco
- ☐ Song Sparrow
- ☐ Swamp Sparrow
- ☐ White-crowned Sparrow
- ☐ White-throated Sparrow

Cardinals, Grosbeaks, and Allies
- ☐ Northern Cardinal

Blackbirds and Allies
- ☐ Brown-headed Cowbird
- ☐ Common Grackle
- ☐ Eastern Meadowlark
- ☐ Red-winged Blackbird

Finches and Allies
- ☐ American Goldfinch
- ☐ Common Redpoll
- ☐ Evening Grosbeak
- ☐ House Finch
- ☐ Pine Siskin
- ☐ Purple Finch
- ☐ Red Crossbill
- ☐ White-winged Crossbill

Old World Sparrows
- ☐ House Sparrow

Barn Owls
- ☐ Barn Owl

Typical Owls
- ☐ Great Horned Owl

Acknowledgments

Thanks to Dr. Andrew Farnsworth at the Cornell Lab of Ornithology for his help and feedback!

To Michael, always—LJA

To my dad, who used to love birds and would have loved this book—MLDG